FATHER CHRISTMAS

COMES UP TRUMPS!

Nicholas Allan

RED FOX

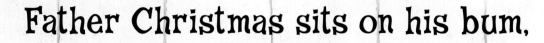

Father Christmas sits on his bum,

It's time for him to fill his tum.

It's Christmas Eve – the night's ahead,

He must be sure he's properly fed.

He eats his dinner – with plenty of sprouts!

"I love my sprouts," he greedily shouts.

Thirty, forty, all smelly and green,

Fifty more . . . and another sixteen.

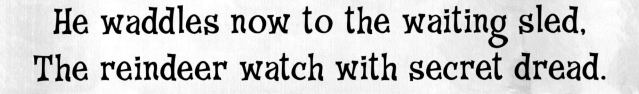

He waddles now to the waiting sled,
The reindeer watch with secret dread.

The sleigh is surely heavy enough
Without this Santa so sproutily stuffed?

INTO the chimney with a SQUASH and a SQUEEZE! –

And through the flue with a PUSH and a HEAVE! And that's when it starts – the first of the trouble . . .

As from his tum comes a . . . **Bubble Bubble Bubble**

"Oh no! Those sprouts! I can feel them start.
My tummy feels funny – I'm going to f . . . !"

"*Sssshhh!*"

says the elf.

"*Don't bottom blow!*"

YOU MUST NOT,

MUST NOT

LET IT

GO!

You'll wake the children and they'll see their toys,
So don't let your tum make another rude noise!"

In the next house he trips – and now he stumbles,
And from his belly comes a . . .

Grumble Grumble Grumble

He feels his way – it's so dark, he fumbles,
And then his tummy goes . . .

**Rumble
Rumble
Rumble**

UP in the sky
and OVER the moon...

UNDER the clouds
and DOWN to the roofs.

In this old house
he slips on a rug,
And from his stomach
comes a ...

Glug
Glug
Glug

There's not much time so on they must whizz,
But the run makes his tummy go . . .

Fizz Fizz
Fizz

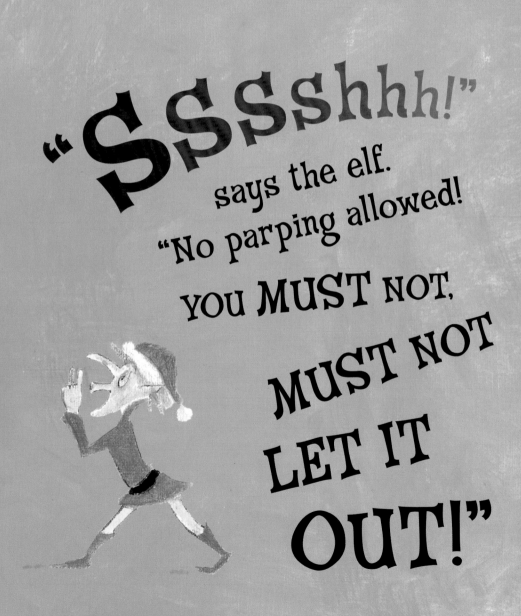

"**SSSshhh!**"
says the elf.
"No parping allowed!
YOU MUST NOT,
MUST NOT
LET IT
OUT!"

The deer are so tired
and the sleigh is so slow,
And all Father Christmas
wants is to blow!

And here is the last child's house in sight,
But no chimney to see in the first dawn light.

So it's . . .

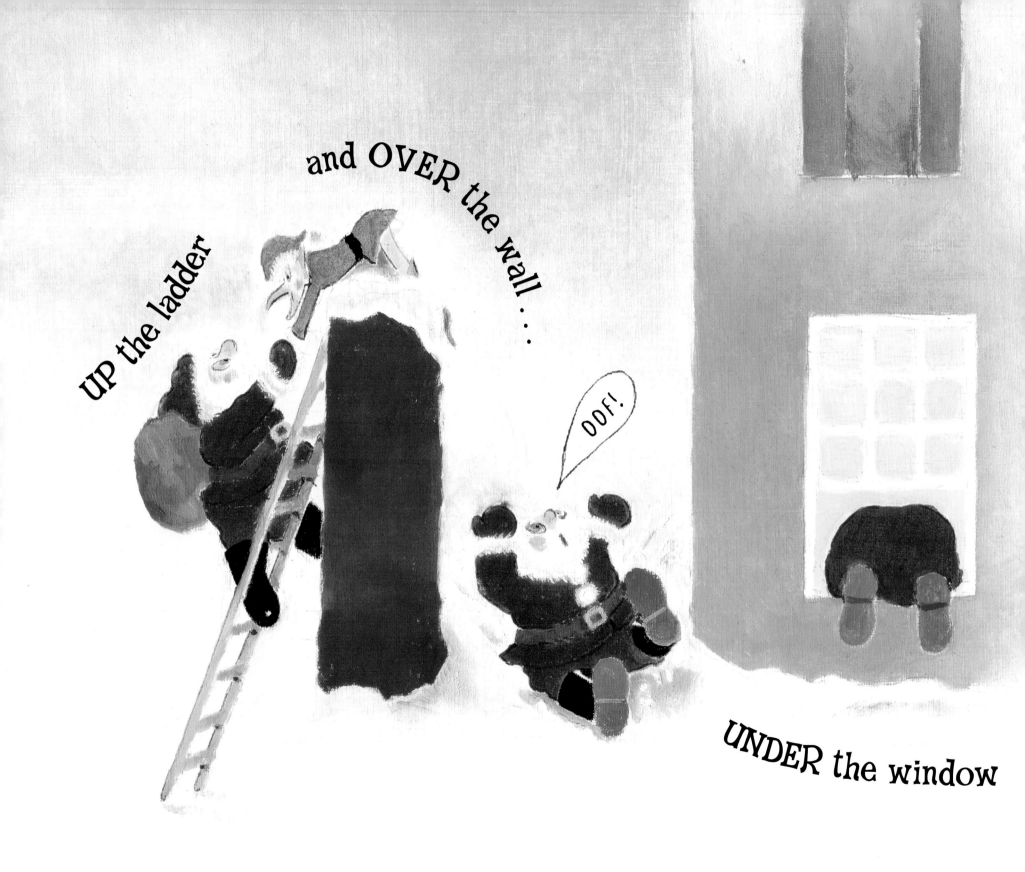

and

Bounce in the hall!

OOF!

But then Father Christmas releases a . . .

And one little child stirs under the sheet!

"Run, Father Christmas!" the elf says. "Run!
And no more rude noises, please, from your bum."

UNDER the window, once OUT of the hall,

UP the ladder and OVER the wall.

But look over here – the deer are so tired,
They lie in the sleigh, completely expired.

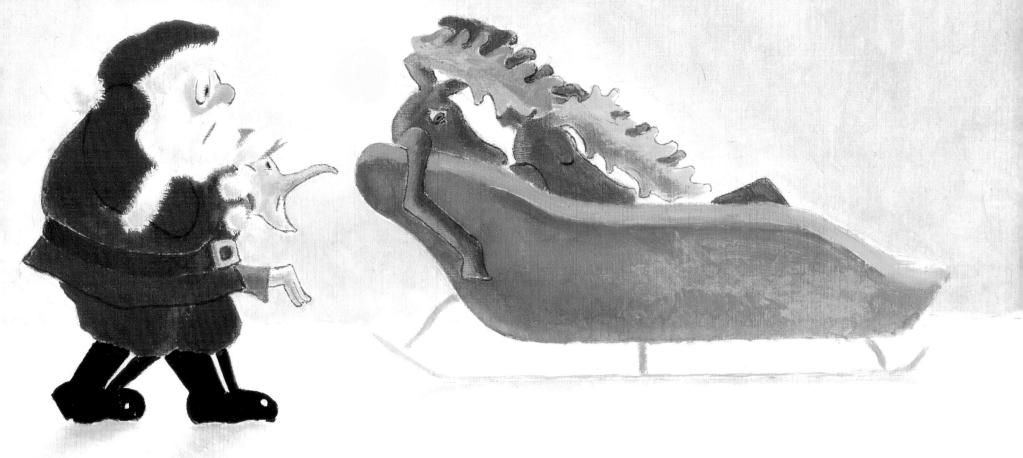

"Now we're all stuck! We can't even depart,
And this time I really **AM** going to f ..."

"Sssshhh!"

says the elf.
"Don't even start!

YOU MUST NOT,

MUST NOT,

MUST NOT   F..."

So the world wakes up,

And the children all cheer . . .

Father Christmas has come up trumps,

North Pole

Now it's the BEST day of the year!